This book belongs to:

_____

To my little princesses, Primrose and Wisteria

This book is based on the TV special "The Prince, the Princess, and the Bee," written by Nadine Van Der Velde,
from the animated TV series *Miss Spider's Sunny Patch Friends* on Nick Jr.,
a Nelvana Limited/Absolute Pictures Limited co-production in association
with Callaway Arts & Entertainment, based on the Miss Spider books by David Kirk.

Nicholas Callaway, President and Publisher
Cathy Ferrara, Managing Editor and Production Director
Toshiya Masuda, Art Director • Nelson Gómez, Director of Digital Technology
Joya Rajadhyaksha, Editor • Amy Cloud, Editor
Raphael Shea, Senior Designer • Krupa Jhaveri, Designer
Christina Pagano, Digital Artist

With thanks to Hannah Bailey.

Special thanks to the Nelvana staff, including Doug Murphy, Scott Dyer, Tracy Ewing, Pam Lehn,
Tonya Lindo, Mark Picard, Jane Sobol, Luis Lopez, Eric Pentz, and John Cvevich.

Library of Congress Cataloging-in-Publication Data available upon request.

Distributed in the United States by Penguin Young Readers Group.

Visit Callaway Arts & Entertainment at www.callaway.com.

ISBN 978-0-448-45023-0

10 9 8 7 6 5 4 3 2 1   08 09 10 11

First edition, February 2008

Printed in China

PRINCE, the PRINCESS, and the BEE

David Kirk

CALLAWAY

NEW YORK

2008

"Hear ye, hear ye; chime the bells!"
A herald sounds the horn.
"We bees proclaim that to our queen
A princess has been born!
Come forth, dear friends, to celebrate
Our radiant majesty.
Both young and old shall soon behold
Our jewel, the princess bee!"

Miss Spider's children stood below
The bustling, buzzing hive,
And found a quiet spot to watch
The royal guests arrive.
"We've stopped to see this noble bee,"
A princess said, "and then
We'll dash to join the royal ball
In far-off Mushroom Glen!"

"The jewel beetle king and queen,
They host it every year,
In hopes the princess they have lost
Will one day reappear."
"But I'm a lost jewel beetle!"
Shimmer gasped excitedly.
"Is there a chance, do you suppose,
Their princess could be me?"
"Oh, you should go," the princess said,
"You look like royalty!"

"The king and queen of Mushroom Glen
Have grieved since we were parted.
They need to find their dear princess;
They must be brokenhearted!"
"I'd take you there," Miss Spider sighed.
"We'd never make it, though.
Not even wings are fast enough—
It's just too far to go."
"That's fine," poor Shimmer sobbed.
"It's just . . . that now I'll never know."

Miss Spider led her child to see
A view from high above.
"Your home," she said, "is Sunny Patch—
The kingdom that we love.
Just look around—this royal land
Helps all our lives to shine
With beauty, friends, and family—
With everything that's fine!"
"This home is lovely," Shimmer sighed.
"I'm just not sure it's mine."

Poor Shimmer brooded by the pond
As froggy Felix swam.
She sighed, "How can I know what's home—
I don't know who I am!"
"Don't worry," said the princely frog,
"You only have to say. . . .
You need a friend to take you there?
I swear I'll find a way!"

Next day, the family surfed the clouds—
A stink hung on the breeze.
Miss Spider pinched her nose and coughed,
"Do I smell rotten cheese?"
"You do, indeed, and so much more!"
A friendly voice implored.
"Come join our cruise to Mushroom Glen,"
Laughed Stinky. "All aboard!"

And as the family made their plans
Who'd make the royal trip,
The princess bee hid silently
And gave her mom the slip.

In golden light the aircraft swept
Above the hills and vales,
With Captain Stinky singing songs
And weaving spooky tales
Of monster spiders down below
Among the bubbling bogs,
Who spit their fire on unsuspecting
Spider kids and frogs!

Our travelers woke—the pungent stink
Of sulfur filled the air.
Through twisted briars,
Great plumes and spires
Of steam shot everywhere.
The great balloon snagged on a thorn;
The rupture blew them past.
To stay aloft the ropes were sheared,
The weights and baskets cast.
Before the gates of Mushroom Glen
They settled down at last.

Miss Spider, Shimmer, Bounce, all dashed—
The ball was starting soon!
The other travelers stayed behind
To patch their torn balloon.
While back within the bubbling bog,
The wind began to moan.
The little Princess Honey Bee
Was lost and all alone.

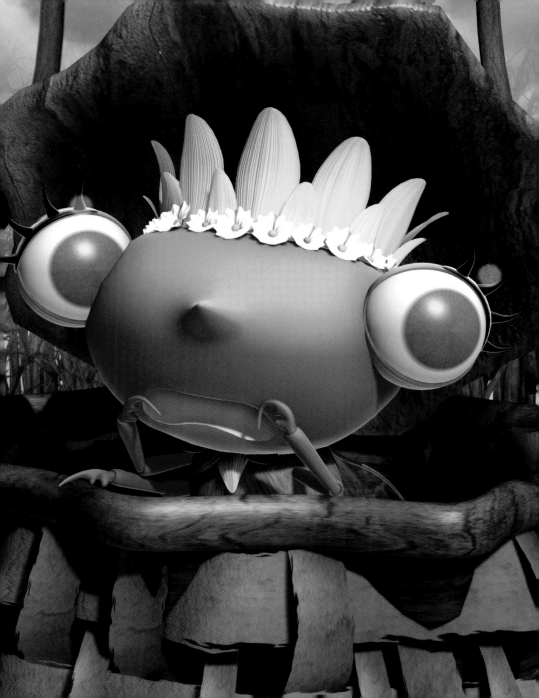

As heralds blew, the gates revealed
A land of emerald green.
Miss Spider's family bowed before
The beetle king and queen.
Miss Spider said, "My beetle girl
Has suffered such distress.
She's come to feel that she may be
Your little lost princess."

There, finally, Queen Beetrice Bee
Reclaimed her precious one.
The beetle queen was moved by what
The valiant three had done.
"Though royalty you were not born,
You've all been brave and true.
Nobility is not in birth,
But in the deeds you do.
"And as reward," the Queen proclaimed:
"A crown for each of you."

"The boys are missing!" Holley cried.
"I'm so relieved you're back—
We need our Shimmer's sensors,
Or we'll never find their track!"
Into and through the murky marsh,
Her sensors led her well.
They found the boys and Honey Bee
And marched back to the dell.

And meanwhile in the Bubbly Bog,
The boys heard someone cry.
Though neither dared to go alone,
They couldn't just stand by.
So princes both, they scorned their fear
And trudged into the muck
To find poor little Honey Bee,
Who giggled at her luck.
But when the three turned tail to flee,
Instead they all got stuck!

The queen took Shimmer in her arms,
And said, "We'll know today.
Please find the tree where you were born.
Fly now and show the way."
So Shimmer let her sensors lead
And landed with a twirl.
"A lovely beetle," sighed the queen,
"And surely someone's pearl.
Our princess, though, was not born here.
You're not our little girl."

"I'm not the princess!" Shimmer sobbed,
"I made us go so far!"
Miss Spider held her close and said,
"I love you as you are."